Up In Fla

by

Hope Wilkie-Summers

For Nan, for telling me to always follow my heart and live my dreams. I love you to the moon and back xx

For Jenson, thanks for helping me with the first chapter

Chapter 1

I re-read the email on my laptop several times. I'd done it. I'd got the job as stage assistant for the local theatre's production of Cinderella. It looked easy. The interview was fun and it got me really excited, I started the next morning.

"Addison!" Mum called upstairs. "Come downstairs for dinner please!"

"Coming!" I called back as I logged off my laptop.

It was just mum and me at home; my Dad had left us when I was a few years old for someone from his office at work. They were married now. I was eighteen and fresh out of college now so that was long in the past for me.

"I got the job at the theatre." I told her as we sat down in the living room, our plates on trays on our laps. "Well done sweetie. Are you sure you want a job this quickly? I mean, you only finished college last month." Concern wrinkled her face.

"Yes, we need the money." That was all that I replied with.

"Addy, you're eighteen! Worrying about money is my responsibility, you need to enjoy life and leave it to me."

Ever since Dad left, I'd begun to notice mum was struggling. Open bills left on the kitchen counter, letters about bank loans opened on her bedside table. It had started to worry me so all I'd wanted was to help mum like she'd helped me my whole life. She didn't want to accept my help, obsessed with putting on a brave face for me. I still saw her struggling.

The next morning, I woke up full of excitement. It was my first day working at the theatre. I wasn't going to wear anything formal, so I chose my black skinny jeans and a pink top.

Mum had already left for work by the time I went to the kitchen to get breakfast. I quickly made myself some toast before grabbing my bag and heading out the door. I locked it before putting the keys safely in my pocket.

The sun was shining and the sky a pale, cloudless blue as I walked to the bus stop. A gentle breeze drifted through my hair. People walked their dogs in the park over the bush to my left, all I could hear was barking. I arrived just in time to get the bus, it pulled into the bus stop as I got there. It was a twenty minute bus ride.

I loved the theatre. It was situated in the town's high street and was next to Poundland and opposite the library. It was huge, taking up a third of the left side of the high street. It had two sets of double doors and a huge poster advertising Cinderella outside of it.

First day. To say the truth, I was really nervous. Plucking up the courage, I stepped through one of the sets of double doors. As I walked through the chandelier lit lobby, I made a mental note to not let anything distract me from this job. What I didn't know was that that was about to go straight out the window.

Everyone was waiting for me when I got to the huge auditorium.

"Sorry I'm late." I called out as I took my seat with the stage manager and director. I knew them both from my interview. Their names were Freddy and Tyler.

"You're not late Addison." said Tyler, the director. "In fact, now we're just waiting on our lead actor." The doors opened as he said that and the actor for Prince Charming came in.

My heart skipped a beat and my breath got caught in my throat.

2

My eyes widened as I took in every detail of him. Black hair, piercing blue eyes, high cheekbones and a smile that could easily melt hearts. It definitely melted mine. He wore jeans and a red t-shirt. I sucked in a breath as he sat in the seat opposite mine. I shifted my attention back to the director.

"Now that Jake's arrived," Tyler said as he looked at Jake "We can begin rehearsals." Lucky for me, the cast had already been decided four weeks ago so people should know most of their lines. Today we were going to begin memorising lines for each scene.

As the actors walked up the steps to the stage, Freddy came over with a basket full of folders.

"These are for you Addy. It's everyone's contact information, all of the casting and everything you need to know as stage assistant." He handed me the basket. Oh my gosh, why were they so heavy? Surely I didn't need all of this. Worst part was that I had to take most of them to and from the theatre every day.

I spent the session reading through the folders. I paid the most attention to the script and everyone's contact details in case of an emergency. At that point, being a stage assistant didn't feel as important as I'd thought it would be.

I looked briefly to Jake, stood in the centre of the stage, before looking away. Alarm bells rang strongly in my mind. Why did Jake seem like a huge distraction? I looked up again for a second and gasped as his eyes locked on mine. I cleared my throat.

The day passed pretty quickly and before I knew it, we were done for the day. I avoided all types of contact with anyone; I needed to stay focused. I kept my head down as I left the theatre. It was a pain carrying all of those folders home. It was starting to drizzle as I walked to the bus stop. Too bad for me that I'd forgotten a coat. I stood under a tree so that I was as sheltered from the rain as possible. The folders were beginning to get soaked so I pulled them closer into me. I stumbled under their weight as I got on the bus.

Mum was getting ready to go out as I got out.

"Where are you going?" I asked as I put the heavy folders on the kitchen counter.

"Not far, just a few drinks with a few friends." She said, slipping on her black flats. "I've left you something in the microwave if you don't feel like cooking for yourself."

"Thanks mum." She kissed my head as she left. I hadn't realised it was almost seven already.

I spent the rest of the evening reading through everyone's contact details. After about half an hour, my phone started ringing. No caller ID. I accepted the call.

"Hello?" I asked uncertainly.

"Addison? It's Tyler." I breathed a sigh of relief.

"Hi Tyler, what's up?"

"I just called to tell you something that I forgot to mention at the theatre."

"I didn't do anything wrong did I?" Panic coated my tone.

"No no no. I forgot to tell you that you'll be working in close contact with Jake. Freddy has a lot to do already as stage manager already, so he'll need you with Jake making sure he gets everything right and remembers his lines."

That wasn't what I was expecting him to say. Working in close contact with Jake every day? I needed to get my emotions in check as quickly as possible.

"Everything okay Addison?" Tyler asked, his voice sounding concerned.

"Yes, everything's fine. I'm just reading all of the information that Freddy gave me earlier." And completely freaking out.

"Oh ok. We've informed Jake that he'll be with you a lot and he sounded really excited about it."

"Oh did he now?" I hadn't thought he'd even noticed me except for that moment when our eyes locked. Apart from that, he'd looked at everyone else except for me. Not that I cared.

"Yes. Anyway, I'll let you go so that you're ready for another long day of work tomorrow." Tyler hung up before I had a chance to say anything more.

It took me a while to get to sleep that night. I was still trying to absorb everything that had happened today. I heard mum get home around ten and I fell asleep not long after.

Next morning I was ready to go. I was looking forward to today's rehearsals. I had a quick shower and a bowl of cereal. I wrote a note for mum on the kitchen counter saying I was leaving early and that I'd see her later.

Full of confidence, I threw open the theatre door and hit something on the other side.

"Ow!" Someone yelped.

"I'm so sorry! I didn't expect anyone to be stood there, are you okay?" I said as I dashed to see if they were okay. Jake smiled at me. Those eyes could make you melt I swear.

"Yeah, I'm fine, no hard feelings. I'm guessing that you're Addison?" I nodded. "Cool, I'm looking forward to spending a lot of time together."

My heart skipped a beat. Tyler was right.

"Shall we go somewhere quiet and look over the script?" I asked as I walked towards a dressing room that I knew never got used.

"Sure." Jake followed me in and closed the door behind us.

5

Chapter 2

I underestimated the size of this dressing room. It was a tiny box of a room with two chairs in a corner and a mirror hung on the opposite wall. Jake and I were sat so close together that I could smell the mint toothpaste he'd used that morning. I was surprised at how well he seemed to know the script. Had he been up all night learning the script like I'd been trying to?

Jake cleared his throat. "So, will you tell me a bit about yourself Addison?"

"You can call me Addy." A blush rose up in my cheeks. "There's not really much to know. Is there anything specific you'd like the answer to?" I didn't know what else to say. I silently prayed he wasn't flirting or trying to distract me from my job.

We spent the next hour asking questions about each other. I learned quite a lot about his childhood and what he enjoyed doing as he grew up. He was an outdoor person; he loved the beach and climbing trees with his friends

After what was probably two hours, Tyler burst into the dressing room.

"Addison, I have a dilemma!" he cried, flustered. His face was white, the look of stress.

"Whatever's the matter?" I asked.

"I need you to be the understudy for Cinderella. We can't find anyone who we think will suit the role, let alone learn all the lines with miraculous speed. As stage assistant, you need good knowledge of everyone's lines anyway. So what do you say?"

My breath got caught in my throat. Me? Act? As the understudy for a lead role? It wasn't exactly what I'd applied for … Although I'd only go on stage if something happened to the original actress.

"Perfect! You've saved me more stress than I'm already dealing with. Have fun working on the script." I swear I saw Tyler wink at me before his eyes flickered to Jake as he left.

I couldn't believe I'd just agreed to the possibility of acting onstage. What on earth was I thinking? The last time I performed onstage was three years ago. It was my Year 11 leaver's ceremony from secondary school. It wasn't the main role, but I was pretty close. As soon as I stepped onto the stage to deliver my scene, I broke down with a huge panic attack. I thought I'd let the team down.

I desperately wanted to have a career in theatre, so I got myself involved in everything. I studied drama at college and was constantly surfing the internet for anything; pantomimes, plays, productions… Literally anything that involved theatre. Then I saw the advert for Cinderella and applied for every backstage role that was still available. Et voila! Now I was the stage assistant and Cinderella's understudy. I just hoped I was over my stage fright by now.

"So you're an actress now too?" Jake joked as I snapped out of my reverie.

"It would appear so. To be honest, I can't really believe that I agreed to it." I explained to him the story of my stage fright.

"You'll be fine Addy, I promise." He smiled and leant in a little closer to me. Our noses were almost touching.

"I hope so."

That evening, I spent the whole time reading Cinderella's parts over and over again. Over dinner, I told mum the news about my understudy role.

"You'll do great. Keep your focus and you'll do absolutely perfect." Were her words of wisdom.

So I'd been up in my room memorising the script ever since. I was getting really good at the first scene.

I'd lost track of the time by the time I finally fell asleep.

I woke up the next morning feeling grateful that it was Saturday. I'd been up into the early hours of the morning working on that damned script. I was glad to have a day to myself; no Jake to distract me. I could get everything done that I needed to, assuming mum didn't make me run any errands for her.

After I'd got up and showered, I decided to cook mum and I fried egg and bacon rolls for breakfast. I'd always loved the sound of bacon as it sizzled in the pan. Once it was cooked, I called mum and she came and sat at the kitchen table.

"I'm going out for a couple hours if that's ok sweetie."

I nodded. "Of course it is. I've got a few things I need to get done anyway."

We said our goodbyes and I went upstairs to my room.

I sat on my bedroom floor with the script out in front of me. My highlighter was on stand-by for when Cinderella came up.

I still couldn't believe that I'd agreed to it. Although I couldn't back out now, I had to get on with it. I spent half of the day memorising and the other half doing housework whilst mum was out. I cleaned the kitchen and did some gardening. Gardening in my words is usually just weeding. I'm not exactly known to have green thumbs. After I'd cooked dinner for myself, mum was still out, I laid on the sofa and began reading my book.

Something was shaking me. I opened my eyes.

"Addy, it's after eight. How long have you been there?" Mum laughed softly.

"I laid down to read my book after having my dinner around four. I must have fallen asleep."

"Go on up to bed. That theatre is keeping you busy, isn't it?"

Mum and I both walked up the stairs, brushed our teeth and then went our separate ways to our bedroom for the night.

The next morning, mum came in holding a stack of pancakes under my nose. They were dripping with maple syrup and had an assortment of blueberries, raspberries and strawberries on top. They smelled so fresh and looked delicious, it was making me salivate.

"Thank you." I smiled gratefully as she handed me the plate along with a knife and fork.

"Enjoy the theatre today sweetie."

I sliced through the pancakes. They were so light and fluffy on my tongue. I ate them quickly then put my plate on my bedside table before heading into the bathroom. I stepped into the shower and felt my muscled relax as the hot water ran all over my body. I kept the temperature as high as it would go, it never burned me. I washed myself with the rose scented shower gel my mum had bought me recently. It was a strong scent but it was perfect for the summer season we were in.

We had 5 months until the show would premiere. 5 months to get everything perfect and all lines remembered. That morning, I swore to myself I wouldn't become distracted by anyone or anything, it was crucial the show went without a hitch. The cast had been selected so there was one less thing to worry about. Our first performance would be in early November and it was just about to become June. Already almost all of the tickets for opening night had been booked.

I stepped out of the shower and wrapped myself in a towel. Within minutes I was dressed and blow drying my hair in front of my bedroom mirror. Perhaps if we all arrived early we'd have longer to work on things, I thought to myself. Everything needed to be perfect.

It was raining when I went outside so I was annoyed at the time I'd wasted drying my hair. I put my hood up on my coat to keep as much of it dry as I possibly could. I knew mum still wasn't keen on the idea of me already working to pay bills, she wanted to be independent and not need help. She'd always been that way. Wind blew strongly as I walked to the bus stop. People swayed as they walked from the strength the wind was pushing at us. Birds were staying in the trees, not flying. I kept a fast pace as I walked. The bus was there when I arrived so I joined onto the end of the queue.

"Can I have a return ticket to town please?" I asked the driver. He had a blue jacket with the bus company embroidered into it and a blue hat on his curly brown hair.

"Of course." I put my card under the card machine and waited for it to beep. He printed out my ticket and passed it to me.

"Thank you." I smiled. I walked down the aisle to find a seat towards the back of the bus. I preferred the back seats so I was away from any screaming children. I found a seat and pulled out the script. Why I was now Cinderella's understudy as well as stage assistant was something I'd never know. I hoped I wouldn't need to act, I had terrible stage fright. I had studied drama in secondary school as a GCSE subject and completely hated it. I'd thought it meant we'd be able to perform and do the backstage jobs as well, but my oh my was I wrong. It was all performance which to me didn't make sense because backstage was the most important role. They were the people who kept everything together and running smoothly, it wasn't just down to the actors. Backstage members are the people who keep everything in line and make sure it's all perfect; the set, whether lines had been rehearsed, giving prompts when needing, blocking the scenes. They were the most important roles and I was feeling so lucky to have a chance to show my skills to everyone. I was a small part of a huge team, but I would make a difference. Just as long as I didn't get distracted.

The last time I'd performed onstage was horrible. It had been for my GCSE assessment. I'd been given an onstage role and denied a backstage one no matter how many times I'd explained how uncomfortable I felt onstage. A few other students studying the subject had been invited to watch the performance. I was full of nerves and anxiety from the moment I'd opened my eyes that day. I knew my teacher knew how badly I didn't want to do it.

"You'll be fine Addy." She had said when she saw how pale I'd become. We were due to start in five minutes. "If I didn't think you could do it, I wouldn't have given you this role."

Shortly into the performance was where it all began to go wrong for me. I was sick halfway through. I'd ran off the stage with the understudy following closely behind me. I was amazed at how I'd gotten to the toilets in time before it came up and I collapsed to the floor in a pile of tears. There were so many faces staring at the stage, it was scary. After that, I knew I wanted a career in theatre, just not one where I wanted to be in the spotlight.

As the bus drove, I turned my attention out of the window. I watched the cars blur past and the wind as it swayed the trees. I heard the sound of dogs barking over the rain pounding on the roof. I put the script away into my bag and kept my gaze outside. I loved the heat of summer, just not the rain. Although where I lived the weather did as it pleased, rather than go off the seasons like it should've. That was the one thing I could never stand living here; the weather. People got on and off at every stop. My spirits lifted slightly when I caught a glimpse of the sun trying to break its way through the clouds.

The driver called out my stop and I pressed the button. The bus came to a stop.

"Thank you." I smiled as I got off the bus. The rain had begun to slow, the sun forcing its presence to be known. Birds were starting to come out, I could see a few flying above me.

I arrived at the theatre still soaked. Almost everyone was already there before I'd arrived. Jake smiled up at me as I walked through the doors to the main backstage rehearsal room. I gave him a discreet wave and sat up near Freddy and Tyler.

"I trust lines are almost memorised?" Freddy called out once everyone was here. "Because today I think we'll start to block the first couple of scenes. Addison, you'll be needed today. Especially your opinion on how you think it all looks."

"Ok." I nodded.

"Shall we get started?"

Freddy and Tyler led us all into the main theatre space and we sat in the rows of seats at the front. The lights had been dimmed.

"Vanessa, please go brighten up the lights." Tyler asked.

"Of course." Vanessa got up and walked to the back of the room. She had a small frame and delicate features. Blond hair framed her face and her hazel eyes stood out against the paleness of her skin. She was wearing a floral patterned dress and small white heeled shoes. The lights brightened up a bit and we began working.

Tyler made his way up the steps to the stage and called up Jake and Cinderella, Lauren I think her name was.

"Addison, while you wait for me to need your support, please look over the script at Lauren's lines."

"Of course."

I got up and walked a few rows back so I could get a little bit of peace to allow myself to focus. I was still feeling really unsure about being an understudy. It had been a few years since my exam performance, but I still didn't think I'd have miraculously gained enough confidence not to get sick again.

They were blocking out the first few scenes for quite a while, I kept peering up every now and then. My excitement lay behind set painting, not being upon a stage. After about an hour, I heard my name.

"What do you think?" The director asked me. "From the top!"

I watched as Cinderella and her father were looking after the animals on the farm when she was younger, I saw a little glimpse into the scene where her father dies. The expressions and body language used really set the tone and showed the emotions being portrayed in the scene.

"I like it. It really shows how happy Ella is in her youth with her father. With the set behind it and the lighting sorted, I think scene one will be perfect as it is." I praised while I silently praying I hadn't dug myself a hole.

"Well if you think so, then I'm sure everyone else will." Freddy said.

"I loved it too! I think we've got the first scene down." Vanessa chipped in. I threw a grateful smile her way and she returned it.

By the end of the day, the first two scenes had been blocked. Tomorrow was set for me to start painting the set. No pun intended. We all said our goodbyes and I decided to head up the high street rather than towards home. The wind streaked through my hair and the sun was slightly covered by clouds. The fresh smell of the sea was carried in the wind. I headed up the high street towards the fish and chip shop. Mum would enjoy a treat.

The high street was filled with shut down shops, charity shops and places like Poundland. It wasn't anything like how I remembered it had been when I was younger. Back then every shop was open and busy all through the day. The market thrived when compared to how dead it was now. People preferred to shop online these days because it was convenient for them, but a community needed everyone to play a part. Nobody did anymore because nobody tried. I didn't have any issues with charity shops, but they aren't the best when you wanted to shop somewhere local for birthdays or Christmas. For that, you'd have to travel to the next town before you found anything.

I grew excited at the smell of fresh chips being wafted towards me. When I was younger, we'd have fish and chips from the chippy every Friday night as a treat. But they became infrequent when the unopened bills began piling up and up. I'd saved my childhood allowance from mum through my teens and only bought for emergencies, so I thought I'd treat mum to an old tradition. A small taste of nostalgia. It was a small take-away shop; no attached restaurant like some chippies have now. I loved the smell of the chips, the fish, the grease and the sausages as I walked in. I breathed in the comforting smell before ordering.

"Hi, can I have 2 small pieces of cod and 2 large chips please?" I asked the lady at the counter. She had dyed pink hair and bright blue eyes.

"Of course. Any drinks?" She asked.

"No thank you."

She called out the order and I heard the sizzling sound of fish being put into the fryers. She bagged up our chips as the fish was lifted out the fryer and drained of the excess oil.

"Salt and vinegar?" She asked as she picked up the salt shaker.

"Salt on one and both on the other please."

She bagged up the fish, put both bags in a plastic bag and handed it to me.

"Ten pounds please." She asked. I held my bank card out and tapped it on the card machine.

"Thank you." I said again as I left the shop. I made my way to the bus station. I knew the food would most likely be cold once I was home, but it's the thought that counted.

As I'd guessed, it was cold when I got home. Mum was upstairs so I hoped the smell hadn't wafted up to her so it could be a proper surprise. I portioned it onto two plates and gave each a three minute blast in the microwave. I knew mum wouldn't complain, she'd just be happy to have a take-away.

"Mum!" I called. "Come downstairs." I heard a groan from somewhere upstairs then the muffled sound of walking. Mum appeared downstairs just over a minute later.

"Yes?" She asked.

"Dinner."

I felt a giant wave of happiness wash over me as I saw her face light up. Her cheeks lifted and she smiled the biggest smile I'd seen her have in years. I never thought such a little thing could bring someone so much happiness. We sat and ate in the living room. We didn't have a dining room; we'd converted it into a study a few years ago. We watched TV with our plates on our laps, a bottle of ketchup on the floor between us.

"Thanks for this sweetie." Mum said and turned to face me.

"It's ok mum, you deserve a treat. It's been ages since we've had the chippy so I picked it up on the way home for us."

"You're the sweetest girl, you really are. I'm so lucky to have you. I'm so so sorry I haven't been able to give you the life you deserve, the childhood you should have had. I wanted to give you so much but I couldn't, whether that was money or time. I worked every spare minute once your dad left us to try to make ends meet and I struggled a lot. I still struggle, as you know. I'm proud of you for getting yourself a job, but once you told me why you'd applied for it, I knew you'd noticed. I hadn't hid everything as well as I'd thought I had and I'm sorry. I haven't meant to worry you sweetie, it's just taken a while to sort things." Tears pooled in mum's eyes and one slipped onto her cheek when she looked up to me. I threw my arms around her.

"You don't need to be sorry, I've loved every moment with you mum. It's been perfect. I got my job as early as I have because I wanted to help so you won't be as stressed out as you have been. You're my mum and you've looked after me so it's my turn to look after you." She still had tears in her eyes when I pulled away.

Chapter 3

It was sunny when I woke up the next morning. I was doing set design today and I could already feel my creative juices flowing.

I still felt sorry for mum after everything she told me yesterday. Even though she was upset I'd got this job to help her, I knew she'd be grateful for it in the long run because it would ease some of the pressure she was under. She needed to know that it was ok to ask me for help. I knew she how much she hated admitting to needing help, but I was her daughter.

She wasn't home when I went downstairs for breakfast, I assumed she'd left early for work. Mum worked in the supermarket in the next town over. She'd struggled applying for jobs after being fired for taking time off after my dad left and that was the only place that had accepted her. Whether or not she liked the job, I had no idea, but I had a feeling she didn't. She never told me any funny things or anything about how her shifts had gone.

I poured myself some orange juice and ate a bowl of cereal. No milk. I couldn't stand milk, I didn't like the taste.

When I got to the theatre, I walked in to pots of paint of all colours in the backstage room. At least I'd get to play around a bit with colours. I found Freddy in the office, his head in his hand.

"Everything ok?" I asked sceptically.

"Our two main actors are late and we can't start without them. Well, I can't start without them. You're on set today so you're fine. Would you mind focusing on that today?" He asked, lifting his head to look at me.

"Of course." I shut the door behind me and headed to the room for set design. I pulled on a painting apron and had a look around. The room I was in was a huge box room, no windows, just a light on the ceiling. Cardboard templates made out the shapes of the castle, already painted and ready for the show. I decided to start with the first scene and began to put together a waterfall. I'd cut the cardboard out and was about to start painting when I heard the door open.

"Wow, you're really good!" Jake exclaimed.

"Thank you. Freddy's looking for you." I replied.

"I know, I'm hiding for a bit." He grinned.

"You'll get into trouble and set the production back." I fretted, picking up a paint brush and glancing at him. He brushed his hair away from his face and sat on the floor next to me. I ignored him and began the first coat of blue for the flowing water. I was using different tones and shades of blue so it looked like the water was flowing. The base of it would be harder, I'd never painted a brick pattern before. Jake cleared his throat.

"How long have you been doing this?" He asked.

"I studied art for four years."

"Wow. You're really talented. Can I help?" He tried to take the brush from my hand, causing my head to snap round. "I did art for a GCSE alongside drama." I couldn't help but notice his eyes sparkle.

"Ok, but stay I the lines I paint for you."

"Aww, it's like colouring when I was five." He laughed and I smiled. I painted the lines for the rest of the flowing water before passing him the paintbrush with the darker shade on it. He took it and contentedly started painting. Almost half an hour passed before Freddy bust in.

"Jake! Where the hell have you been?"

"Helping Addison paint. Prince Charming isn't in every scene you know." He winked at me.

18

"No, not every scene, but he is in the one we're trying to work on. Please come help us, you can help Addison in a bit, I don't need you for too long." He sighed.

"Ok." Jake began to get up. "Here you go Addy." I swear I felt a high voltage of electricity pulse through my veins as his fingers accidentally touched mine. I blushed as I took the brush from him. I felt something in me drop when he closed the door behind him.

No no no. No distractions. Not again. I'd gotten distracted by a boy at my last job and ended up fired. It was in retail which I hated anyway, but it was a job nonetheless. It still earned me money. I'd worked there for almost a year and he'd started three months before I was fired. I'd been asked to train him, which proved to be difficult when he kept looking at me with bright blue eyes behind his dark hair. He always wore a strong smelling aftershave and I always knew when he was around. I watched my actions more when he was around so I didn't embarrass myself. We hung out often after shifts and went out for dinners regularly.

I'd been asked to set up a new display when Jamie walked past me. The strong waft of aftershave knocked me off my feet and I felt like I was up in the clouds. I wasn't. I ended up losing my footing on the ladder I was on, fell off and knocked down half the shelves on the aisle with me. My manager stormed over to me and sacked me on the spot. I completed the final hour of my shift and afterwards me and Jamie sat in the park. The sun was setting and we were lying in the basket swing together. His arms was wrapped around my shoulders, my head on his chest.

"I'll miss you on shifts." He whispered.

"Me too, but I'll still see you. I'm not moving away." I laughed, snuggling into him.

"I know."

It was that moment. My first kiss. At sixteen. My pulse was racing through my veins, my breath short. Jamie leaned his head to the side slightly and pressed his lips to mine ever so gently. He cupped my cheek with his hand and I put my hand on his shoulder. His lips caressed mine. It felt like fireworks were going off in the sky behind us. His body twisted to face me and he pulled me closer. I gasped as his tongue traced mine once before it pulled away. We were out of breath when we broke apart. The sun was setting, the birds flying into their trees.

It was over after our kiss. Jamie moved away to London just over a month later for college and he rarely answered my calls. It was after that that I promised I wouldn't fall in love again with someone I worked with. The aftermath was too painful.

I pulled my focus back to the flowing waterfall. After a couple more coats it would be perfect. I picked up the bottom bits and took off the lid of the grey paint. I was going to try grey stone bricks with moss and ivy. Fingers crossed it would look good. A few hours passed with nothing but me and my background music. I was about to stop for lunch when the door opened again.

"Hey, I got you lunch."

"Oh, thanks Jake. I didn't think you'd be done for another couple hours?" I could hear the confusion in my voice.

"I'm in all of five minutes of the scene they're working on. Lauren isn't doing too well today." He shrugged. I put my paintbrush into the pot and gratefully accepted the McDonald's he handed to me.

"Thank you."

"I didn't know what you'd like, so I kind of got you chicken nuggets." I glanced at him and he looked sheepish.

"They're my favourite."

We sat on the floor and ate our food. I ate mine quickly because I needed to get back to work.

"Do you ever take breaks?" He laughed when I picked the brush back up.

"Only when I'm not the only set designer around. Besides, the more I do it, the quicker it'll be done."

"Then let me help." He put the rubbish in the bin and put on another apron. "I'll finish the water for you." He began adding more coats of paint to the water while I outlined the bricks for the bottom. I wanted it to be perfect. Jake seemed really happy I'd let him help me so I asked him to help on the bottom once he'd finished the coat he was doing.

"Do you fancy dinner tonight?" he asked.

"Where?" I asked, thinking whether it was a good idea to go against my rules.

"Anywhere you like." Wow. Freedom.

"Sure, we'll have a walk around later and choose somewhere."

"Ok."

I wasn't doing anything bad, was I? Colleagues go out for dinner together and drinks all the time. Nothing had to happen. It wasn't a date.

I was full of anxiety for the rest of the day. I couldn't stop wondering about dinner would end. I couldn't bear another work romance like mine and Jamie's, especially when he moved away and cut me off. It was agony.

It was relatively dark when we finished up for the day. I shivered into my jacket as we stepped into the cool evening air. Jake put his hand on the small of my back and guided me towards the top of the high street. We had a few decent pubs and restaurants near the theatre, I wondered which one he was taking me to.

"So do you know where you'd like to go?" He asked.

"Nope. You can choose."

"You sure?"

I nodded in response. We walked up towards the nicer pub, the more expensive one. Laughter radiated from inside. It was hot as we walked in. He put his hand on my back again and gently guided me to one of the far corners. We sat in a booth that was more closed off than the others.

The pub was painted green and gold for the interior. Paintings of various paraphernalia were hung up on the walls to add colour and decoration. The chairs in the booths were made from leather, the other sets of tables and chairs were wood. The floor was wooden floorboards, lamps hung around the walls. There was a bar near the entrance door to the pub and it was very crowded. I picked up the drink menu before passing it to him.

"What would you like?"

"A gin and lemonade please. Cherry gin if they have it." I requested.

He got up from the booth and made his way to the bar. My eyes dropped to his backside before flicking back up to look at the bar. So many thoughts were buzzing around in my mind, like bullets being shot. One straight after the other. I shook them off when I saw him walking back over carrying two drinks. I smiled as he placed my gin and lemonade on the table in front of me. I picked it up and took a sip.

A waitress came over to our table. Her hair was blond and short, she had brown eyes and her uniform was messy. She wasn't wearing it overly neatly. She was holding a pen and order pad.

"What would you like to eat?" She asked, looking at Jake. I could see the lust in her eyes and a blush was slowly spreading across her cheeks.

"I'd like a burger and chips please." Jake asked, his deep voice sending goosebumps up my arms.

"Sure." She replied, barely audible. "You?" She asked, but kept her eyes focused on Jake.

"Pasta please." She noted it down, took our menus and headed off to the kitchen.

I picked up my drink and had a few long sips from it. Jake had his eyes focused on mine as he waited for me to speak. I didn't. He cleared his throat.

"Set design seems fun." He pointed out.

"It is, it's the reason why I love being backstage. Everyone in the audience always thinks that the actors painted it when it's actually the people you never see during the performance. Being backstage is like the stitches in clothes, it keep it all together." I explained, feeling a little more confident.

"It sounds better than being onstage. I like being the lead actor because of the attention, but I'm never confident when I'm up there. I get ignored by my parents at home so theatre feels like the only way to get people to pay attention to me." His eyes clouded over as he spoke as if he was lost in thought.

"I'm sorry to hear about your family."

"Don't be, I'm used to it now." Jake sighed. "Tell me about you."

"What would you like to know?" I asked, the corners of my mouth lifting.

"Your interests, family life, career choice, hobbies. All of it."

"Well, at home it's just me and mum. My dad left us when I was little and he left mum to struggle. It became a regular sight to see unopened bill envelopes on the kitchen table because she couldn't bring herself to look at the amounts inside. So after leaving college last year, I got this job so I could help her pay the bills, although she hates that she's technically the reason why I got job straight out of college." I stopped talking as our waitress arrived with our food. Once again she kept her gaze fixed on Jake as she put our plates down.

"Anything else you'd like?" She asked him. Jake ordered another round of drinks for us both. She went to go get them.

"I think it's great that you're trying to help your mum out. You're such a good daughter."

We talked and drank for about another hour before we decided to call it a night. I was feeling tipsy and wobbled slightly as I walked. Jake slipped his arm around my waist as he slowly walked me home.

"Thanks for tonight." I slurred. " I loved you. It. I meant I loved it."

He laughed softly. "I loved it too. Rain check for another night?"

"Definitely."

Chapter 4

A few weeks passed and production was going well. Jake and I had been out for a couple more meals together, occasionally with Lauren and Vanessa. Tyler was becoming concerned about Lauren, she was becoming withdrawn. I'd gotten a lot more set ready and Jake had managed to memorise all of his lines.

We were getting closer to our performance date and I needed to pull my focus back. It had strayed to constantly dreaming about Jake and it needed to stop. We'd blocked most of the scenes and were focusing on lighting. Costumes were being made, set almost completely finished. It was shaping together quite well. But the next Thursday morning, all hell broke loose.

"Lauren's quit!" Tyler cried. Everyone stopped what they were doing and turned to look at him. "She's called and said she's quitting. Now what are we going to do? Our lead actress is gone." He slumped into a chair. Jake nudged me forward.

"Addison is her understudy, she can do it." I was going to kill him.

"Of course. Don't worry folks, crisis averted. Thanks Addison."

I felt my jaw drop. How could he do that to me? And why? He knew my fear of being onstage, I'd told him that during one of our nights out. Yet he had to go and backstab me. Prick. We went back to what we'd been doing before Tyler had burst in and I felt someone nudge my arm.

"At least now I get to kiss you." He whispered before walking away. Holy shit. Jake had done that because he wanted to kiss me. I felt the heart of a thousand burning stars course through me and I fully took in what he'd said. I really needed to finish memorising the lines. I wasn't convinced I'd be a good Cinderella.

After a week of close contact with Jake onstage, I'd given up trying to stay away. If I fell for him, then so be it. I could already feel myself falling for him. How could anyone not?

"Dinner tonight?" He asked between scene transitions.

"I'll meet you outside the main entrance." I grinned.

We were working on the final scene, the kiss scene. Tyler had suggested we work on the last few scenes as I'd watched the first being blocked.

Lady Tremaine descended the stairs. "Oh look daughters of mine, the prince is here!"

"I want to be a princess!" Anastasia wailed.

"No, me!" Shrieked her sister. There was a knock on the door. Both girls squealed in excitement. Lady Tremaine crossed the stage to the door and opened it to the Duke.

"Evening, by request of the Prince, all ladies of the household are required..." He began.

"Yes yes do come in."

Both girls were sat on the couch, waiting for their turn. In the meantime, Ella was locked in the basement, but able to hear each word.

"Oh I do wish there was a way out of here." I said as I began to pace back and forth. "They need to know it was I who danced with the prince, not my step sisters." I pretended to play with my skirt as the costumes weren't quite ready.

"Very good." Praised Freddy. "Then your animal friends give you the key they got from upstairs and you unlock the door from inside and rush upstairs to your Prince."

I unlocked the door and made my way to the sitting room to join my step-family.

"What on Earth are you doing?" My step mother yelled. "Oh ignore her my Prince, she's just our servant, she doesn't need a turn."

"Oh I believe she does." Jake replied and winked at me. I felt my face turn crimson. "Please, sit."

I sat down as instructed and lifted one leg over the other. Jake knelt in front of me and took off the shoe I was wearing. He slid on a white heel in its place.

My step family gasped in shock.

"It fits! My Princess, I've found you. Come to the palace and be my Queen and rule with me."

I took a deep breath because I knew what was coming next.

"Of course I will!" I cried. Jakes hand slipped round my waist and pulled me in close to him.

"You're my happy ever after." He whispered and his lips softly brushed against mine. Adrenaline pulsed through me and I parted my lips slightly. His arm gripped me tighter and I lifted a hand to his chest. His smell was intoxicating, as was his kisses. His lips were so soft and gentle against mine. My fingers worked their way up into his hair and it did indeed feel as though it was happily ever after.

"Great work!" Shouted both Tyler and Freddy as they clapped.

"We'll rehearse the wedding scene as soon as Addison's dress is made." Said Freddy.

I looked up at Jake and he was looking at me. "I told you." He smiled. I blushed before Vanessa pulled me off the stage.

"Nora is after you for your fittings."

"Oh great."

Vanessa led me down a lot of hallways before we reached the Costume Design room. The door opened onto a room filled with various fabrics shelved on the walls. In the middle of the room was a wooden platform with a mirror behind it. Fabrics of floral patterns were strewn across the floor with an older lady scrabbling to pick them up.

"Hi Nora." Vanessa called. Nora looked up and smiled at us. "I've brought you Addison."

"Ah the princess to be." She laughed. "Come here darling, I just need your measurements for now." I waved goodbye to Vanessa and headed over to Nora.

"Where would you like me?" I asked.

"On the platform please my dear." I began to step up onto the platform but she stopped me. "I'll need you to be in your underwear dear so I can get the measurements right."

I slowly took my clothes off, keeping a watchful eye on the door. Who knew when someone might walk in?

"I lock the door during fittings." Nora said as though she'd read my thoughts.

"Ok, thank you."

I stepped onto the platform, holding my arms around myself to try to keep warm. Nora moved to various positions around my body and I shivered every time her cold measuring tape touched the heat of my skin.

"Are you alright with strapless, dear? Tyler wants the wedding dress to be strapless."

"Yeah, I'm alright with them. Do the others have sleeves?" I asked in return.

"More or less." She responded. Her wispy grey hair kept flitting into her eyes. After around ten minutes, she walked back around to my front. "You're all done dear."

"Thanks Nora."

I jumped off the platform and pulled my jeans back on, trying to balance on one leg.

"Do you need me to grab anyone else for you?" I asked as I opened the door to leave.

"Not yet dear, you best get back before they send a search party." She laughed as I closed the door. I navigated my way back to where everyone else was waiting for me. A scarlet wave overtook my cheeks when I saw Jake. The kiss we'd shared before I went to Nora. I knew it was part of the performance, but the way he kissed me made me feel as though it was a little more than that. God only knew I couldn't wait to kiss him again.

I took myself off to do more set designing for the afternoon. They'd hired someone else for my old role so I wouldn't be drowning in my work, it had definitely lifted a weight off my shoulders. I knocked on the door.

"Yeah?"

"It's me."

"Oh, I suppose you can come in."

I laughed as I opened the door. Stefan was crouching on the floor, covered head to toe in paint a glitter. His blond hair was streaked with different colours and so was his face. His green eyes stood out against his pale skin.

"You look like something from a Picasso piece."

"Oi you cheeky bugger!" He shot back as he turned around to face me. I picked up another paint brush. He was working on the wedding scene, the set for the church already partially completed. The thing I'd begun to learn about Stefan was that he never worked in a logical order. Where I'd left him with the first four scenes done, he'd moved to making the pieces of set for the last few scenes.

"Do you want any help?" I asked.

"That would be great. Although shouldn't you be kissing Prince Charming?" He mocked.

"Jake. And no because I kissed him earlier." I giggled.

"I bet that got your tongue tied. He is rather easy on the eyes, isn't he?"

"Yes." I replied, feeling a blush stretching its way across my cheeks. My face was admitting to the crush I still needed to keep under wraps.

"Are your dresses pretty?"

"I haven't seen them. I've just had my dress measurements done so that Nora can begin to make them."

"I bet your wedding dress will be gorgeous."

"Me too." I felt myself beginning to daydream so I snapped my attention back the task at hand.

We finished for day quite early. It was Friday, Tyler's favourite, so that could've been why. I didn't feel like dinner with Jake tonight, I wanted time with mum. A girl's night in. Birds were scouring the streets for crumbs of food.

Mum was cooking when I arrived home. I locked the front door behind me and followed the smell into the kitchen.

"Hi mum." I said as I hugged her from behind.

"Oh hi sweetie. I wasn't expecting you yet, aren't you going out with Jake like you often do on Fridays?" She asked as she turned around and held me back.

"We finished earlier than I expected today and I don't fancy diner with Jake today. I would like a mother-daughter night." I proposed.

"We haven't done that in ages!" Mum exclaimed. "Let's cook dinner together and have a girly pamper night."

Mum and I made ourselves pasta. She fried the mince in an oiled saucepan whilst I cut the onions and carrots to mix in with it. Mum put the pasta into another saucepan with boiling water. I was careful with the knife I was using because our kitchen was tiny and mum kept walking to the sink to drain off the excess fat and oil. I added the onion, carrot and sweetcorn to the mince. Mum left me with the saucepan while she washed up in the sink. When the vegetables were cooked, I opened a jar of Bolognese sauce and tipped it in. I stirred it so that everything was coated in the sauce. Once the sauce was finished, I waited for the pasta. Two minutes left.

"I love cooking with you. We used to do it all the time when you were younger." She reminisced. The timer beeped so I moved the pasta to the sink and drained it through the sieve.

"Me too."

Mum had laid bowls out on the side so I dished up both our dinners. As mum poured some orange juice while I carried both bowls through to the living room. Mum put the glasses on the coffee table and put on the TV.

"Is the production going well, dear?" Mum asked.

"Yes, the scenes seem to be going quite well. We began working on the scene where she gets her shoe back and they kiss in happiness." Oops. I forgot I'd told her I was now Cinderella.

"Oh so you kissed Jake today then?" The cheeky smile she gave me the beginning of a blush to form.

"Yes." I said as I hung my head. Mum grinned like the Cheshire Cat, ear to ear. She made a weird squeak sound and I peered up at her. "Let's finish dinner and have a pamper night. No more questions about Jake or his kissing antics.

"No more questions about Jake and his kissing antics." Mum repeated.

Chapter 5

We spent the evening in my bedroom, doing facemasks and stuffing ourselves with popcorn.

"Have they found a replacement for you yet? You can't be lead actress and backstage at the same time; they're both very time demanding roles." Mum asked, concern in her eyes.

"Yes, someone called Stefan. He's lovely. When I'm not needed anywhere then I sneak away and do set design." She smiled in response and began to peel off her face mask.

It was after ten when mum suggested I go to bed.

"Goodnight mum."

"Goodnight sweetie."

When I was tucked in bed, my mind drifted off to how Jake had kissed me. How soft his lips were, how caring. How gentle he was when he'd held onto me. Was I excited for him to kiss me again? Did it mean anything if it's just a performance rehearsal?

A week later, I wished I'd been ten minutes later getting there than I was. If I'd been late, I wouldn't have heard the conversation I had. The conversation that had led to me crying in the backstage toilets.

I arrived at the theatre before most people. I was early, ridiculously early. I was walking to the dressing rooms to talk to Nora when I saw two people talking around the corner. I took a few steps backwards before they saw me.

"What on earth do you mean? She's doing great given the circumstances." One voice said sharply. Jake.

"She's not fit for the part. Or pretty. She should be behind the scenes, unseen from everyone where she belongs." A female voice. I knew that the actress of one of the sisters was praying to earn the Cinderella role once Lauren had quit, but I'd got it instead. "Addison had no reason to be Cinderella."

"No, Tyler and Freddy are loving her performance though. She has earned everything she's got from here."

"She's not good enough, Cinderella's supposed to be pretty, that's why she becomes a princess." I had a feeling it was the actress of Anastasia with him. I peeked round the corner and saw them stood closely together. Jake was backing against a wall as she walked closer to him. She put her hand on his shoulder. "I bet she's not even a good kisser."

He threw her hand off him. "Get off."

She drew even closer, their chests almost touching. "If I'd got the part, I could make you feel so much more than her. I'd kiss you so gently," She pressed him against the wall. "Then after the show, I'll take you home. Back to my place, strip you down and we'd fuck late into the night. You'd make me scream your name over and over…"

I never heard the rest, or Jake's reply. I turned around and sprinted at full speed to the toilets. Which was how I ended up locked in one crying for however long. I lost track of time. Tears flooded down my cheeks, the wetness blurring my vision. I sat curled up on the floor in the stall I'd locked myself into. I knew Jake had defended me, but she'd pushed it way too far.

I was alerted shortly later on by someone calling my name.

"Addison?"

I sniffled and didn't respond. The bathroom door opened. "Addy? Oh Addy are you ok?" So she'd seen the closed cubicle door then. "Honey open the door."

I slid back the lock on the door and Vanessa pushed it open slightly. Seeing my face, she walked into the cubicle and pulled me in for a hug. "Everyone's waiting for you."

"Ok." I wiped my nose at the back of her sleeve and peered up into Vanessa's concerned eyes. Her hair was up in a ponytail with a small plait running through part of it. She held out her hand and I took it as I heaved myself up.

"We'll clean you up and then we'll go in." Vanessa led me to the sink and began running cold water from the taps. It trickled out slowly at first. She wetted some of the handtowels stored above the sinks and slowly washed my face. The coolness of the water cooled down the swelling and puffiness of my eyes after all my crying. I dried my face on my sleeve.

"Let's go." I gave her my best smile.

"That's the spirit, Addy."

We walked side by side to the main room of the theatre. Everyone's attention snapped to us as we opened the doors. Jake's expression conveyed shock.

"Are you all right?" Freddy asked as he began to get up.

"Yes I'm fine," I croaked, "Please stay sat and carry on."

I sat in the row in front of Jake. I could feel his eyes staring into my skull from behind. I concentrated on Freddy. Tyler didn't appear to be present this morning.

"We won't be doing any scenes today. With Tyler not here today or tomorrow, we'll all be focusing on our costumes and set design. Stefan and Addison can help if you have questions for the set pieces. Nora will call for people throughout the day for fittings or measurements and anything regarding your costumes. We've told her how we'd like them, but Tyler and I agreed to give you a little freedom to make a couple changes." Freddy paused. "Vanessa I'd like your prompts and views on lighting.

Everyone else to set design please. It needs completed. Thank you."

We all got up and went to set design. I found my piece from the wedding scene I'd started and Jake joined me. I remained silent until he spoke.

"Are you alright? I saw you crying earlier." "His voice sounded thick with worry. Did I tell him what I saw or did I just leave it? Before I could comment Anastasia came over.

"Hey Jake," She purred, her voice filled with lust. She began to wrap a hand round his neck but he swatted it down. "Wanna paint with me?"

It looked as though he glared at her. "No Tara, I'd rather stay with Addy. Work with Stefan." Jake turned around so he was completely opposite me and his back was to her. Tara huffed before storming away. Again.

"I saw you two earlier." I said out of the blue a few moments later.

Jake ran his hand through his hair. "Did you? Did you hear anything?"

"I did. I heard you defending me and shutting her insults towards me down; I thank you very much for that. I also saw her push you to the wall and saying what she'll do to you…" I trailed off.

"So you didn't see me push her off and say my heart is elsewhere?" He questioned, looking at me dead in the eyes.

"No, I saw that and ran away after deciding I'd seen enough." I focused back on my work. He lifted my chin with his little finger.

"It lies with you." I felt my jaw almost drop.

"M-me?" I stammered.

"Yes. I've like you since our first meal out. You might not have, but I saw every meal out when it was just us as a date." Jake confessed.

"You did?" I asked, doubt creeping into my tone.

"Yes." He explained, exasperated, as he ran another hand through his hair.

"Oh." Our eyes locked, I slowly released a breath.

"Addison and Jake." We both turned our heads to find Nora holding a clipboard and pen. She had a measuring tape draped around her shoulders and was wearing a blue cotton dress. "Can you come try on your final scene costumes please? Stylists are waiting."

Jake and I stood up and followed Nora to the dressing rooms. It was a huge room with mirrors and chairs in stations down one side. Clothes rails were along the far back wall. I took a peek at all the costumes and gasped at Cinderella's wedding dress. The dress was like a ball gown. It was strapless, the bodice made with silk and little flowers were embroidered into it. The skirt was tulle and flowed out around the bottom; it was gorgeous. I couldn't believe I would be wearing something as beautiful as that dress. No way would that look good on me, I thought.

"Dressing rooms are behind you both." Said one of the stylists. Her hair was in a pixie cut and was dyed in two colours: half pink and half blue.

"Thank you." Jake and I said in unison.

"Would you like help changing dear? The dress might be difficult for you to do up." Suggested Nora.

"Please."

Jake went into one changing room as I followed Nora into another. She carried my dress as though it belonged to a queen, gently and gracefully. She undid the dress while I took my jeans and top off. She placed the dress gently on the floor and I carefully stepped into it. We pulled it gently up my body and I twisted around so she could do up the back. I was in awe at the pattern on the bodice. The dress pushed my boobs up a bit, I wasn't sure if it was good or not. Nora pulled back the dressing room curtain and I stepped out and walked to the styling chairs.

Jake was already changed into his navy blue tux. He was jaw-dropping gorgeous at that moment.

"You have such beautiful hair." Pixie girl said as she brushed through it. She brushed all the knots out before plugging in a curling iron. My eyes opened wider, I didn't like my hair curly. "Don't worry, I'm only going to curl the ends and see how that looks."

I nodded meekly.

Keeping my head still and straight for as long as I did was painful. I wanted to steal peeks at Jake but couldn't without my stylist complaining. After an hour, we were done with my hair. A tiara was placed upon my head with a long veil attached to it. I got up and looked at myself in the full height mirror.

"Wow, you look beautiful." Jake said, coming up behind me. "You really look like a princess in the wedding dress, Nora did an amazing job." He rested his hand on my hips and I sucked in a breath. My hair was down, curls on my shoulders.

"You do look rather handsome. " I blushed as I pulled my hair over one shoulder.

"Thank you."

Nora took a picture of us both in our costumes and then asked us to change. We changed back into our normal clothes and then began walking the long walk to the set design room. Jake clasped my hand unexpectedly and I gasped. I looked up into his eyes and watched his smile from ear to ear.

"You are really, very beautiful." Jake took a step towards me. His eyes dropped to my lips for just a second and I parted them. Slipping a hand round my waist, he slowly lowered his lips to mine. I felt my body ignite as he kissed me. I rested a hand on his shoulder, another round his neck. We drew back for breath for just a second and then he pulled me back in. I felt his tongue trace my lower lip and my mouth opened a little wider, just enough for him to slip his tongue in. My body shivered in shock at the touch. I pulled away.

"We need to go. We should be working." I whispered, his nose touching mine and our lips almost locking again.

"They won't even know we aren't there." He flirted, placing a delicate kiss on my nose.

"Mm Tara will."

"I don't care for Tara. She's obsessive, been after me for the whole three years since I met her, yet she continues to ignore me when I say I'm not interested." He laughed and I let out a small laugh too. Our faces were still touching.

"It still hut to see this morning though."

"Would you rather you were in her place at that moment?" He pressed his lips to mine again. I nodded slightly when he drew back. "Thought you might." He grinned.

"Let's get going."

Jake laughed and let me through to the room with everyone else. I went back to the wedding flowers I'd been drawing. I was making arches with leaves and roses. I was going to put glitter on the roses so that they would stand out in the lighting. If Jake didn't keep distracting me, then my vision would be perfect if it looked as good as it did in my head. Tara was glaring at us from her corner with Stefan. I smiled back at her.

I sketched out the design of the roses and the leaves. At the moment, it looked like random lines and zigzags. I got a big pair of scissors and began cutting around the outer leaves that made the arch shape. I then mixed some paint together to create a light shade of green. I painted the leaves as Jake painted another set piece. I waited for the green to begin to dry slightly before paining the roses. I coloured the red and pink on the tips of each petal.

Hours passed before everyone had finished. I was sure it was late evening. We all filed out of the theatre, finished for the day. Jake swept up behind me and took my hand. He led me up the high street and I assumed we were going for dinner. I was filled with confusion when we walked past the pub.

"Where are we going?" I asked becoming increasingly more confused.

"To the club."

"Oh?"

It was loud when we arrived, the sound of the bass music could be heard from three roads away. A long queue of people were lined up at the door, two very large, tall men stood outside dressed in full black.

"Jake, are you sure about this?"

"Yes, trust me Addy, it'll be fine. You do have you ID with you though, right?"

"I never leave home without it."

"Good."

We joined the back end of the line to go in. The music was really loud, would I really enjoy this like he seemed to think? When we eventually reached the front of the line, the bouncers stamped our left hands and allowed us in. Bright lights and even louder music awaited us inside.

"I'll get us drinks, what would you like?"

"I'll come with, it's too crowded for me to feel safe left alone." I followed him up to the bar.

"What will it be?" Asked the bartender.

"Rum and coke." I asked as I looked at Jake.

"Two rum and cokes." Jake requested. I watched with curiosity as the bartender made up our drinks. He was so swift in making them and barely spilt a drop. He handed them both to Jake and we left the bar. We took a table at the edge of the dancefloor and drank our drinks.

"Productions going well." He stated.

"Yes it is. It's only three weeks until our opening performance. I'm really anxious."

"Don't be."

"Why?"

"Because you're perfect for the role, you deserve the role. You're a perfect Cinderella." I smiled, a blushing spreading across my cheeks. He took my hand. "You have nothing to worry about."

We drank a few more drinks and then made our way to the dancefloor. Taylor Swift was playing and Jake took my hand and made me sway to the music. Bright blue and pink lights circulated the room. We danced our way through lots of songs before Jake slightly pulled back.

"I'm going to the toilets. Keep dancing and I'll come back."

I watched as Jake walked towards the toilets and I took to the floor again. I wasn't dancing much, I didn't want to embarrass myself whilst I was alone. Two hands held onto my hips and I picked up speed thinking Jake had returned. Soft kisses were laid on my neck with hot breath soothing my skin. I wrapped his hands around my waist and pressed my back against his chest.

"Well aren't you getting down." A gruff voice slurred in my ear. I instantly dropped his hands and turned to look at the guy. He had blond hair and hazel eyes, eyes that were glazed over. I tried to step away from him but he held onto my wrists tightly. "Where are you going, babe? I'm not done yet."

"Please let me go." I said, trying to pull myself away again. He tightened his grip.

"Let her go!" Thank God Jake was back. Jake wrapped a protective arm around me.

"She your girl?" The stranger asked.

"Yes." Jake replied.

"Sorry mate, didn't know." He said and walked away.

Jake turned to me, his eyes searching mine. "You ok?"

"I am now thanks."

"Drink?"

"Please."

I was more than drunk by the time we left. I couldn't walk straight, Jake held my waist the whole way out the club. We were both drunk, me more than him.

"Can't go home." I slurred, tripping slightly. "Mum will kill me."

"Stay at mine." Jake pounced.

"Ok."

We slowly made our way to Jake's flat. The moon shone down on us, basking us in a silver glow. His flat was small, a one bedroom place. His lips were on mine as soon as he'd closed the door. I tangled my fingers in his hair and pulled gently, receiving a soft moan in response. His tongue traced my lips. I gently bit his lip and felt electricity surge through my veins. He picked me up by my thighs and I instinctively wrapped my legs around his waist. He carried me through to his bedroom.

Jake's room was clean, for a guy. The walls were blue, he carpet grey and a double bed was on the far wall. He threw me onto his bed and I giggled.

He climbed on the bed, on top of me, and placed slow, gentle kisses down my neck. His hot breath was making my skin start to tingle.

"You're so hot baby." He groaned.

I felt myself begin to pant under his touch.

I was starting to feel myself sobering up as I lay on the bed, closed my eyes briefly and discovered the room didn't start spinning.

His hand slipped under my shirt and began exploring my bare skin underneath. With the other hand he lifted my shirt up over my head. His eyes popped as he took in the sight of me in my bra on his bed. His lips crashed down on mine and he began unzipping my jeans. Pulling them down, he moved and kissed down the length of my thighs and I moaned with every hot kiss and my back arched off the bed. He threw my jeans to the other side of the room. I sat up and pulled off his shirt and he grazed his lips against my chest. I felt pressure begin to build in my lower stomach. I pulled him up and our lips locked.

He pushed me back and took his jeans off so he was wearing nothing. I laid myself back down on the bed. I gasped as I saw how ready he was for me, so so ready. His fingers stroked down my stomach and slipped under my pants. Gently he pulled them down. My breath quickened my pulse racing through my veins.

"Oh Addy, you're so gorgeous." He moaned as he kissed my stomach. I winced at the pain of him slipping a finger inside me. He repeatedly laid kisses on my thighs and I found myself filled with such a level of pleasure that I had never before felt in my life.

"I want you Jake." I whispered.

"Ok baby," he purred, "You can have me." He pulled my pants completely off and lifted me higher up towards the pillows. He climbed on top again and I felt his want for me press into my thigh. I was as ready for him as he was for me.

I needed him.

Reaching inside his bedside drawer, I heard the sound of foil. *Oh shit.* He took it between his teeth and tore it open. I averted my gaze to the ceiling as I felt him roll the condom on before pressing his lips to my neck.

This was it.

He stroked me before I felt him slip inside me. A wave of pleasure took me over and then a tiny sting of pain. My body was remembering this feeling from years ago.

He was so slow, so gentle. He was caressing every inch of skin, every little part of my body as he kissed me all over. I'd never been touched like this before, not by any other guy I'd dated. Jake was so intimate with every touch he laid on my body, every searing hot kiss he gave me.

We fit each other perfectly like two puzzle pieces.

I moaned as he pulled himself out a little before strongly pushing back in.

"Is this ok?" He panted. I didn't say anything, I just gazed into his eyes and nodded.

His lips locked on mine and I opened my mouth so he could taste me. His tongue played with mine as his hand pressed down on my stomach. Holy shit, the things he was making me feel. He pressed down on my stomach, making me squirm and moan and the pressure that became more intense. My eyes rolled to the back of my head.

"I can feel you getting tighter." He moaned in my ear. He began to pick up his pace of sliding in and out of me. I bit my lip, trying to hide my pleasure. His lips grazed my neck and he sucked it gently and I was done. I felt myself come undone all over him. He moaned loudly in my ear.

He thrust himself into me harder, causing me to whimper. I watched the muscles on his shoulder strain.

"That was amazing." He panted. I stroked my fingers through his hair, his sweaty face pressed to the soft skin on my chest. I smiled and gazed up at him. He wrapped an arm round my shoulder and we closed our eyes and fell asleep.

Chapter 6

I woke up in a strange bed. Where was I? I heard a grunt next to me. Cautiously I looked next to me. Memories from the previous night flooded my brain as I saw Jake next to me. I remembered how we'd ended the night. My blushing increased as Jake rolled over and his face rested on my shoulder. I carefully got out from the bed and covered myself with my hands. I found my clothes strewn across different parts of the room. My head was pounding from the alcohol from last night.

I padded through the flat to Jake's kitchen and put the kettle on to boil. Looking around, I found a small pot of hot chocolate and put a few spoonfuls into a mug. I poured in the boiled water in and stirred. Topping it with squirty cream from the fridge and sat in the living room. After watching TV for a bit, I heard the bedroom door open. Jake yawned and met my eyes. His hair was dishevelled and his eyes sparkled the sunrise at new dawn. Beautiful. He'd put oxers and a t-shirt on before leaving the bedroom.

"I was surprised to find you weren't still lying next me when I woke up. Are you ok?" He asked as he sat beside me.

"Yeah I'm fine, I just needed a drink. Would you like me to make you one?"

"You're in my flat Addy, I should've made for you because you're the guest." He deadpanned.

"I don't mind honestly." I really didn't mind, but it felt nice that he wanted to do things for me. He got up and boiled the kettle again. He made a coffee, black, and came and sat back next to me. He wrapped an arm around my shoulders and I snuggled into him slightly. Then his phone rang.

"Hello?" He asked.

"It's Freddy. You don't need to come in today, Tyler's still off and I've got a stomach bug. I'll call everyone else and let them know." Freddy's voice croaked down the line.

"No need to call Addison, she's here with me so I'll tell her." Jake smiled at me.

"Ok, enjoy your day off."

He put the phone down.

"What was that?" I asked.

"We have a day off. Freddy's sick and Tyler isn't in either. So we can spend the day together again." He purred and leant closer so his lips met my nose.

"I'm down for that." I grinned.

"Great!" He lips met mine and I felt myself melt into the kiss. His arm held my tightly around my waist, keeping me close to him. I lifted and hand to his shoulder. We broke apart to catch our breath.

"What would you like to do today?" He asked, stroking my cheek.

"Something fun." I responded. He placed a kiss on my forehead before retreating into the bedroom, presumably to get dressed.

I wondered to myself what today would bring as I took another sip of my drink. His coffee was still steaming on the floor by my feet. He didn't have a coffee table. Maybe he was treating today like a date? If he was, I was even more excited for today.

Jake came back out some time later, hair wet and fully dressed. He was a sight to behold. I felt myself falling further for him, even though I hated to admit it. Last night I'd felt more alive than I had since I could remember. Feeling his hot skin against mine, feeling how much he lusted for me through kisses… It had been blissful. Last night had been perfect, a night I'd think of for ages. I wanted to live another night like it, but did Jake? Had it meant as much to him as it had for me? I turned my attention back towards Jake.

"Are you ready?" He asked.

"Where are we going?"

"Hop in my car and find out." Winked Jake.

I picked up my phone from the sofa, put my shoes on and followed Jake into the lift. The doors closed and we were alone. We didn't utter a word the whole ride down.

It was a gorgeous bright morning. Clouds were dotted through the sky, the wind casted a gentle breeze. Jade green leaves from the branches, the crisp smell of morning filling the air. Birds flew around, people walked dogs and cars drove by.

Jake produced a set of car keys from his pocket.

"This one." He said as he pointed to a red Audi. The paint on the car sparkled in the sunlight. It looked almost brand new. He unlocked it and opened the passenger door for me.

"Wow." I gasped.

The seats were leather and carried its distinct scent with it. The car had a masculine feel about it. He had a jelly bean air freshener hanging from his rear view mirror. I clipped my seatbelt in and he started up the engine.

"I never knew you could drive." I acknowledged.

"That's because I'm within walking distance of work and I like the exercise. I don't tend to drive unless it's a long journey."

"So this is going to be a long car ride?" I asked as he gently reversed out of the parking space he was in. He turned left onto the main road and we were off on our little adventure. He hadn't told me where we were going and I was so tempted to ask. I gave in.

"Where are we going?"

"A place you told me you've always wanted to go to."

Well that narrowed it down, but not by much. There were lots of places I wanted to go. But which one was he taking me to?

"Hmm." I thought absent-mindedly. "That could be Devon, Brighton and Cornwall. Lots of places. Do I get a hint?"

"Not at all Addy. Nice try." Jake laughed.

A short time later I think I must've fallen asleep from the relaxed pace on the road. I opened my eyes and saw a sign that said Brighton in ten miles.

"Brighton!"

"Oh so you're awake now."

"Sorry." I yawned.

"It's ok, we were up later last night than you're probably used to."

"Yeah, but I wouldn't change it for the world." I whispered.

"What was that?"

"I said that yeah I'm not used to late nights like last night."

"Ok, we're not far now."

"Good because I need to pee."

"Want me to stop somewhere?" He asked.

"I can hold it until we stop, keep driving."

He changed lanes on the motorway and hit the accelerator. I opened my window and we were hit by the wind as we wove our way through other cars. I felt a feeling of freedom with Jake. Not just when I was in his car, but when I was simply spending time with him.

I felt free to do whatever I wanted to when I was with him. I looked back to last night. I wouldn't have done that with anyone else, I didn't have the self-confidence but I had thought that another guy would take one look at me

47

and walk away. Jake had so gentle, so intimate. *Too intimate.* He'd made me feel things I'd never felt before. Last night was a night I'd treasure for a long time.

Jake and I arrived in Brighton and it took a long time to find a place to park. He began to find "Just Keep Swimming" as I watched him slowly become wound up by how busy it was. I was going to say something, but then changed my mind because I didn't think he'd find it helpful. I watched his frown turn into a grin as he found an empty spot. A little dimple showed, something I'd never noticed before.

We got out the car and I was in awe. We could see the beach from where we'd parked. It was so sandy, the ocean a bright blue and I couldn't wait to cover my toes in the sand.

Noticing my smile, Jake asked "Where first baby?"

I felt my heart skip a beat at him calling me "baby."

"Not sure, beach looks gorgeous though." I began taking careful steps in its direction.

"Like you."

I felt myself blush uncontrollably.

"Race you!" I called and took off running.

"Not fair, you had a head start!"

We ran through the people on the pavement. Some sent me confused looks but I didn't care. He'd remembered a place I'd always wanted to visit and he'd driven us the couple hour drive to get here. I was so happy. I saw him catching up as I looked out the corner of my eye so I increased my pace as the pavement became empty in front of me.

"I'm gonna win." I chanted, grinning ear to ear.

I did, in fact, win.

"Oh no. I lost." He laughed.

"Yep, and you owe me an ice cream as a reward to me for winning."

Jake rolled his eyes. "Fine. But I'm getting myself one. You can have a double scoop. I need to cool off after that running."

"Deal."

We wandered down the beach. The sand was soft between my toes; I'd taken off my shoes after our race. I felt the sun radiate its heat on my chest. Jake reached out my hand and slowly hooked his fingers between mine. My fingers twitched but I held onto his hand. My hair was a mess after running, my forehead was beaded with sweat. Jake's hair was wind-blown and his skin glowed.

We eventually came to a little café on the beach. It was just off the esplanade, it's foundation on the sand. It had a patio spreading out onto the sand with a couple of table on it with the sun umbrellas up. A few people were sat outside, more queued up at the ice cream window. The café had small windows and not much room inside. It appeared to be mostly ice cream and beers. We joined the queue for ice cream.

"Still allowed two scoops?" I asked, swaying myself side to side in plea.

"Yes."

"I wonder what flavours. I hope they hope they have my favourite."

"And what would that be?" He asked, raising his eyebrows at me.

"Cherry and chocolate."

"I'm not a fan of cherries, but that sounds lovely."

I took a glimpse at the ice cream cabinet. There were so many. Bubblegum, candyfloss, cherry bakewell, rhubarb and custard, parma violet; the lost went on. I hadn't knew half of them were ice cream flavours.

Surprised, I said "There's so many."

"Well you can pick two or one."

"Definitely two." Who knew an eighteen year old could be so excited by ice cream? I didn't, but I clearly was excited. I felt like a child when your parents take you into a sweet shop. So many choices, but not allowed everything you see. I wasn't paying attention to anything until I felt Jake nudge my ribs.

I stepped forward.

"A scoop of mint please." Requested Jake. He looked at me.

"A double scoop for me please. One cherry bakewell, the other rhubarb and custard please."

The lady behind the counter scooped up Jake's, put it in a cone and passed it to him.

"Cone or tub?" She asked me.

"Uhh tub please."

She passed mine a minute later. Jake handed over the cash and we thanked her as we left. I took a spoonful of cherry bakewell and slid it into my mouth. My mouth came alive at the sudden burst of cherry flavour. There were broken biscuit pieces in it too. I took a spoonful of rhubarb and custard. My tongue tingled at the sourness of the rhubarb but it then relaxed as the sweetness of the custard stole the sour taste away. I loved it. I loved them both.

I peeked up to Jake to see him biting away at his. Mint. Such a classic flavour for a guy to have.

"Shall we sit on the beach?" He asked.

"Please."

Jake found a vacant bench a little farther down the beach. Moment after I'd finished my ice cream, he took my face in his hands and kissed me. I felt fireworks go off like I had last night. Everything was perfect. I sucked in a breath and put my hand on his neck. I took his bottom lip between mine and gently sucked before letting go. It drove him crazy, I felt him tense beneath my touch.

He stroked my cheek and kissed my nose, my lips. His face was close to mine, his breath against my chin. I leant forward slightly and kissed him gently before he took my hand and led me down the beach.

Was I starting to fall in love with Jake?

Chapter 7

The sun stayed out all day. My excitement rocketed up as I found an arcade. Jake was taking photos of the beach as we walked. I slowly sneaked backwards whilst he wasn't looking and crept towards the arcade.

"Jake!" I called, unable to bear him thinking he'd lost me. "I'm going to the arcade I found." I said as he jogged to catch up to me.

"Go for it. I'll meet you in there."

I jogged briskly to the arcade. It was massive. 2p machines, claw machines and child games filled the massive room. In a closed off part was the eighteen and above gambling machines. I had no interest in going on those.

I searched the claw machines to see if there was anything I wanted to win. I came to one with cuddly animals in it. A white fluffy polar bear caught my eyes and I set my target. I inserted a few pounds and made my attempts to catch it. It dropped it a few times near the prize drop box but it never fell in. A hand landed round my waist.

"Which one you going for?" Purred Jake.

"The polar bear. The stupid thing keeps dropping it." I huffed. I tried again and it almost made it. I threw my hands up in exasperation.

"Let me try. Take a tenner out my pocket and go on a different game." Jake said as he took my position at the machine controls.

"Which pocket?"

"Back." Oh.

"Ok."

I slipped my hand into his back pocket and I felt him tense beneath my touch. I slowly took my hand out his pocket once I'd gripped the only note in there and stroked him with the back of my hand as I took my hand out his pocket. I turned around and just about felt him leave a quick kiss on the back of my head.

I wandered over to all the 2p machines in the middle of the arcade. Most of them had keyrings inside, some had little toys in. I found one that had keyrings saying "I heart Brighton" on them. I searched around for a money converter machine and converted the tenner pound coins, and the five pounds into 2ps.

I began playing for the keyring and was surprised when I shortly caused an avalanche.

"Yes!" I cried and blushed as Jake looked over to me with a grin on his face. Bless him, he was still trying to win me the polar bear.

An hour passed in which I'd won two Brighton keyrings; one for each of us to remind us of today. Mine was already attached to my house keys. I went back to find Jake.

"I have three quid of yours back." Jake was focused on the claw, still holding the polar bear, dragging over to the prize box. It didn't drop it. We both jumped with joy. Jake leant down to pick it up.

"I believe this is yours." He held it out to me.

I hugged him. "Thank you so much!" I took it from him and cuddled it to my chest.

"Are you going to name it?"

"At some point, when I think of the perfect name." I suddenly remembered the keyring. "Oh yeah," I said as I fumbled around in my pocket. "This is for you. I have one as well and I thought we could both have one to remind us of today. I got it in the 2p machine."

He took it gratefully. "Thank you Addy." We looked into each other's eyes longingly. My stomach growled.

"What time is it?" I asked as I clutched my monster roaring stomach. Jake took out his phone and peered at the time.

"Time to get dinner and then drive back home. Shall we?" He asked, holding out his arm and putting on a posh accent.

"We shall." I giggled, taking his arm.

We looked on Google maps to find a nice place for dinner after leaving the arcade. There was one that looked good about ten minutes away. Jake led the way towards the centre.

I knew I was lucky. I was lucky to have been treated the way Jake had been treating me and he'd made me feel special. Some people don't ever get to experience the fireworks moments I'd been having and I was so grateful to have them.

The sun was beginning to set, the orange and pink colours in the sky creating a beautiful pattern. I was in awe. I'd had a perfect day. I'd ticked a place off my bucket list. Even though we'd spent the day on the beach and in an arcade, it had still been perfect.

The pub we ended up at was called The Frog and Mouse. It was an unusual name. We went in and found a small table tucked in the corner by the bar. I wouldn't be having alcohol tonight. The carpet was red, the bar was big and well stocked. It was fancier than your regular pub, polished tables, fluffy carpet, expensive paintings on the walls.

I leant forward in my seat and picked up the menu before Jake had a chance to. I watched as he slouched in his seat while my eyes scanned the menu. I made my selection before passing it to Jake. After a few moments he beckoned the barmaid over.

Her brown hair was plaited and tied into a bun on her head. She was dressed in all black.

"What can I help you with?" She asked politely.

"We're ready to order our food and we'd like two lime sodas please." Oh did we now Jake? I couldn't remember telling him what drink I'd like.

"Of course, I'll send someone over for your food order."

"Thank you." I said. I stared across the table at Jake, who was grinning like the Cheshire Cat with his little dimple showing. Our waitress was blonde and she had blue eyes. Her hair was in a ponytail.

"What can I get you both?" Her eyes were focused on Jake.

Jake gestured to me. "Ladies first."

I cleared my throat. "I'd like tomato pasta with a side of garlic bread please."

"Yep." She said, her attention still fully on Jake. "You?"

"Steak please. Medium rare. With chips."

"Is that all?" She batted her eyelashes at him. I sat smugly in my seat, safe in the knowledge his attention was on me.

"Yes." He said and she took our order through to the kitchen. The barmaid returned with our drinks.

"If you'd like another drink, call me over."

Jake smiled. "Thanks."

After she left, we sat in silence again. Why did it feel like there was tension in the air now? We'd spent all together in blissful happiness but now we were doomed to silence for dinner. What was going on? I shifted in my seat and turned my focus to the paintings. Most of them looked pre historic, some were from battles. They all looked expensive, that was one thing I was positive about.

"I've enjoyed today." Jake said, cutting into my thoughts.

"So have I." I replied, turning back around to face him.

"It's been special because it's been with you."

I didn't get to respond because the blond waitress bought our food over. She laid them on the table and stopped to stare at Jake. He gave her what, to me, looked like a glare and she skulked away.

"Bon appetite." He smiled, holding up his fork.

I stabbed at my pasta and took a mouthful. The flavours were strong and intense. And hot. Too hot. My tongue was on fire. I started choking and had to launch my hand at my lime soda. The cool liquid put the fire out. I looked across at Jake, my eyes watering.

"Oh don't worry, I'm fine." I wiped at my eyes.

"I know."

I rolled my eyes at him and picked up more pasta, this time blowing it. I dipped my garlic bread into the sauce once I'd eaten all the pasta. Jake had finished before me and struggled to hold in his laughter when I looked at him.

"What?" I snapped.

"You have sauce on your face." He leaned forward and wiped tomato sauce from round my mouth with his thumb. I watched intently as he sucked the sauce off his thumb. I picked up my drink and downed the rest of it.

"Dessert?" I asked, leaning towards the menu.

He snatched it away. "When we get home."

He walked over to the bar to pay the bill. In the meantime, I got myself ready to leave.

"I'll meet you at the car." I called. I didn't know if he heard me, I hoped he had. I waited by the Audi, my arms around my body to keep warm. The car unlocked and I got in.

Jake had the radio on the whole ride home. Music filled the car to take away the unwanted silence. Once we got on the motorway, Jake put his hand on my thigh and squeezed it gently. Butterflies erupted in my stomach.

"Are you staying at mine tonight or am I dropping you home?"

"I'd like to stay at yours please." I saw him smile.

It felt the ride home was longer than it actually was. We just about made it into the elevator before I had his lips on mine. I smiled against his lips. I pressed one gentle kiss to his lips and stepped back.

"Addy." He groaned.

"Wait."

"Fine." He took my hand. He crashed his lips on mine again once he'd closed the flat door. This time I didn't resist. I parted my lips for him, giving him more of me to kiss. He scooped me up and took me into his room. He gently placed me on the bed, not breaking this kiss. His hand stroked my waist, my fingers in his hair. He was knelt in front of me. His hand snuck beneath my shirt and he pulled it off. Jake trickled a trail of kisses from my ear, to my neck, to my collarbone.

"Jake." I gasped.

"It's just kisses, don't worry. Not like last night."

His lips went past my chest and to my stomach. I felt the butterflies coming back. I yawned. Jake looked up at me.

"You're tired, we'll go to sleep."

"But I was enjoying that." I sighed.

"I saw you yawn. We have work tomorrow anyway." He got up off the door and left the bedroom. I heard the bathroom door close. Did I just ruin that? Had I upset Jake? Pushing my negative thoughts aside, I took my jeans off and climbed into the bed. Jake came back a few minutes later in his boxers and switched off the light. I turned onto my side so I would be facing away from him. Something thumped into the bed.

"Oof."

"There's a bed there." I stated.

"Thanks Addy, I had no idea." Jake laughed. I heard him patting his way up the bed until he found the pillows. He settled into bed behind me. I snuggled myself up under the duvet. Jake shifted to get comfortable.

"Addison?"

"Yes?" I whispered.

"Can I hold you?"

"If you wish."

Jake snaked his arm around me and I moved back slightly so we were touching. My ass was on his stomach, his bare chest hot against my back. He wound his hand up to my chest and rested it there. I sucked in a breath. He must have noticed because he dropped his hand to my stomach. My breathing evened out. I felt his hot breath on the back of my neck.

I turned over to face him. I smiled into the darkness and brushed my nose to his.

"Don't push it." He murmured.

"I'm not."

"Trust me baby, you are."

Did I want to do this? The answer was a firm yes. I stroked his cheek and left a gentle kiss at the corner of his mouth. His jaw stiffened. His hand gripped onto me tighter. I placed a delicate kiss on his chest. I rolled onto my back and closed my eyes.

Chapter 8

I was woke up the next morning to something tickling me. Was it a stray hair on my neck? I batted at it.

"Ow." Oops.

"Sorry."

"Remind me never to wake you up with kisses again." Oh god, his voice was so deep in the mornings.

"Can I have a shower?" I asked, rolling over to face him. His eyes sparkled.

"Of course. Quick though, we need to go soon."

Groaning, I got out of bed and padded to the bathroom.

"Towel?" I called.

"Use mine. Blue one."

"Ok." I closed the door and locked it. No way was he sneaking in.

I ran the water. It blasted out cold but then slowly changed to warm water. My muscles relaxed as the hot water soothed them. I washed my hair with the apple shampoo I found in a bottle at the bottom of the shower. I stood there for a few minutes longer just to let the water soothe me. Turning the water off, I stepped out the shower and wrapped Jake's blue towel around me.

I walked through to the bedroom. My clothes had been neatly laid out on the bed, along with a pack of pants. Had he really just run to the shop while I was in the shower? I got dressed and went out the bedroom. Jake was in the kitchen, spreading jam over some slices of toast.

"Nice shower?" He asked as he handed me a plate with toast on.

"Yes thanks. What flavour?" I asked looking at the toast.

"Raspberry."

Checking the time on the clock above the kitchen sink, we inhaled our breakfasts and made a run for the elevator. I wasn't sure about Jake, but I hated being late anywhere. Clouds covered the sky when we got outside and it was cold. Not what you'd expect in summer, was it? People were on their morning walks, some rushing to make it on time to the bus.

Barely anyone was at the theatre when we arrived. I breathed a sigh of relief. Jake chuckled next to me. We sat next to each other in the front row of seats as Tyler came in.

"Hello you two. Enjoy your day off?" Quizzed Tyler.

"Yes thanks. I took Addy to Brighton for the day."

"I loved it." I chipped in.

"It is lovely there, I went a few years ago myself." Tyler reminisced. More people start filing in and I saw he was getting ready to start. "Freddy will be in later." He announced.

A few people muttered between them.

"We only have two weeks until our opening performance. I'm so proud of how well all of you are doing so far. I'd like to work through the script scene by scene for final checks that it's all perfect. Nora needs some people for costume checks, Jake and Addison are the only two she's completely finalised with." He paused for breath. "Can everyone who's dancing in the ball go to see her please?" A lot of people got up and left. As they were just extras for the ball scenes, I didn't know any of their names. Tyler called up the actors he needed for the first couple scenes. Jake and I stayed put in our seats, our legs ever so slightly touching.

We watched Ella growing up, and we watched her grieve with her father when he mother passed away. If I hadn't have seen this scene multiple times before, I might have cried a little It was so upsetting to see a young girl lose her two parents within three years of each other. My dad walking out on us had been hard enough. Tyler had changed the story slightly so that Ella was raised by the house staff after her parents died. I wasn't a big fan of his script change, but it would do. Hopefully the audience liked it instead.

Soon enough it was time for some of the scenes with me in. We worked through each scene with ease, having already rehearsed over a million times. Well, it felt like a million. With every movement I made, I was beginning to feel my stage fright slowly slipping away. *I could do this.* I was going to perform as Cinderella in two weeks' time and I wouldn't freak out or get sick. My confidence in myself was beginning to lift. I'd come so far since my GCSE days.

When the extra people had come back, we ran through the ballroom scene. Oh how good it felt having Jake holding me. I'd longed for it all day, but we hadn't snuck a moment together. He had a hold on my waist with one hand and held my hand up with the other. We waltzed around the centre of the stage. It felt as though it was only the two of us there, dancing our way to happiness.

The set for every scene was complete and perfect. It fit every scene exactly, the ballroom pieces were gorgeous. Tyler had opted to use the fountain I'd painted for the castle garden as well as in the wedding scene.

The run through went well, Tyler was really proud of it.

"End of the week we'll do a costume run through." He said to us.

I couldn't wait to put on my wedding dress again, I'd felt so good in it. Jake had complimented how good it looked on me and I couldn't wait for him to look at me that way again. Next week couldn't possibly come fast enough.

All of the step sister's dresses had been fitted again and were now ready. I'd had so much fun today, I couldn't wait to go home and tell mum all about it. I'd kept her updated on where I was the last two days I hadn't been home. She was buzzing about how I'd been with Jake all weekend, she'd be like an excited puppy when I told her the details over dinner that night.

We were finished before the evening after two run-throughs. Freddy didn't turn up in the end, I wondered if he was alright. It was dusk when we left. I meandered down each dark street on my way home, figuring out what story to feed my mum. I'd leave out the events from after the club visit. I reached my street and she pounced on me as soon as I unlocked the front door.

"Tell me everything!" She squealed, hugging me. Sometimes my mum wasn't the adult she was supposed to be.

"Ok ok. Let's cook dinner and then I'll tell you." I laughed.

We made ourselves burger and chips. Mum had been trying to eat our way through the freezer for months. We made ourselves comfortable while we ate.

"So tell me." Mum said through a mouthful of beef burger. "Did he treat you well?"

"Yes, he took me to Brighton yesterday and we had the best day." My eyes lit up as I replayed the memories of the past few days in my mind.

"How lovely, you've always wanted to go there, haven't you?"

"Yes. We went to an arcade and had a beach day and went back to his flat."

"And did you share his bed?" Oh God. Now I was doomed. I could either deny it, or she'd find out later. I had two options and I didn't know which one to take.

Mum surveyed my silence. "Sweetie I just want to check you're safe and well."

"I'm fine." I whispered picking up a chip and dipping it in tomato sauce. She eyed me inquisitively.

"So did you?"

I nudged her. "Muuum. But out!" I laughed. "If I ever need advice or help I'll definitely come to you."

We made eye contact and burst into laughter. She used to push me for details about the boys I was with but I think she's slowly backing off as I grow up. She hadn't pushed me much about Jake so there was progress already.

Dress rehearsals were horrible. Some actors picked at their costumes or were too bothered about them to actually focus. It was our first dress rehearsal, and the last rehearsal before the show. I was so nervous to be going onstage. Performing in front of the cast was ok because mistakes were always made in the production process. It was a whole different story in front of an audience. My name would be in the programme beneath my picture so everyone would know my name and face. What if I messed up and everyone in the town made fun of me?

I made my way to the theatre slowly, still lost in my thoughts. I was late. Late because I hadn't set an alarm like I was supposed to; I just hoped I wouldn't be in trouble. I knew I would be the last one to arrive. I silently prayed that I wasn't desperately needed at that moment. I had the folders in my bag that I'd been given on my first day, I figured it was best to bring them back to give to Stefan, my stage assistant replacement. It really did feel like I was lifting weights at the gym. Struggling, I opened the theatre door to join everyone else. All eyes turned to me as I stepped in, making loads of noise as I managed to whack the folders against the door.

"Addison."

"I'm sorry I'm late. I did try calling." I stammered.

63

"Yes and I got your message. Please join us."

I waddled down to sit with everyone else. Tyler cleared his throat and Freddy continued talking from where he was before I'd interrupted.

"Dress rehearsals are the most important. It's the one where the director's vision is brought to life. It's the final check that all costumes are ok so costume designers know if any final work needs done before the big day. It's an important day. We'll be focused mostly on lighting today."

He looked at Vanessa.

"Vanessa, we need to find a sequence for the ballroom scene. It needs to be pretty and different colours so it may take a while to finalise a sequence that goes well."

"Got it, I'll start on that straight away." Vanessa said and she got up and made her way to the lighting box at the back of the hall.

"The rest of you are free unless Nora needs you and until I need you."

I stayed sat where I was. Jake rose out of his seat and sat next to me, resting a hand on my thigh.

"Are you alright?" He asked.

I rubbed my forehead. "Not really, I'm not feeling too well." I replied.

"Stay here." He got up and left.

I turned my attention to the stage, where the extra dancers were practising. They twirled around countless times. The lights changed through a sequence of different colours. There were blues, pinks, purples.

Jake returned a short while later carrying a bottle and a small box. He passed me the bottle.

"I went and got you paracetamol."

"Thanks." Gratefully I took two tablets from the strip he passed to me. I swallowed each one with a sip of water.

"Just think, it's only a week now until our first performance." He whispered.

"I know, I'm so nervous." I fretted.

"You'll be great. I know you will." He left a delicate kiss on my temple. My body turned to jelly beneath his touch. He ran his hand through his hair, damp from a shower. My head was pounding, my vision starting to blur around the edges. I closed my eyes then opened them again. "You ok?"

I got up out my seat, thinking walking would help. I tripped coming out the row of seats; then everything went black.

Chapter 9

I came to and found myself in a strange room. There were cushions beneath me and a blanket over me. The room was tiny, barely any form of decoration. I could hear someone breathing nearby. I gently opened my eyes.

"Thank goodness you're alive." Vanessa was sat on the floor by my side. Her eyes were full of concern. "Drink this." She passed me a glass of water.

"Thank you." I took a few sips and felt the col liquid rush down my throat. I went to sit up and she put her hand on my back.

"Easy, you had quite a fall."

"I wasn't feeling well, what actually happened?" I asked groggily.

"Jake said you got up out your seat and tripped. Although it looks more likely that you fainted." She slowly helped me sit up. My heart palpitated for a few moments then resumed beating as normal. How long had I been out of it? I asked just that.

"About half an hour."

"Jesus."

"Yeah, but as long as you're ok."

"Where is everyone?" I rubbed my eyes.

"Final checks for everything."

"Jake?"

"Onstage probably, rehearsing and worrying about you. He freaked out when you fainted."

"I need to see him, tell him I'm ok. How did I get here? And where are we?" I asked, my mind confused and only just registering the fact that I was no longer in the main theatre.

"Jake carried you out; we're in a backstage room that never really gets used. Thought you'd want the privacy when you woke up."

"Thank you. I really appreciate that."

Vanessa helped me to my feet and we slowly made our way back to the main hall. Discreetly, I opened the door, with Vanessa's help and shuffled in. Jake jumped off the stage and launched himself into my arms. He held me in a strong, supportive grip and I snuggled my nose into his neck. He pulled back.

"I was so worried about you." He murmured looking me dead in the eyes. I felt my knees become jelly at how his eyes sparkled. He pressed a kiss on my forehead. "Are you okay?"

"Yes thanks. I'm ok. Thanks for carrying me to a quiet room; it really helped not having everyone in my face."

"No problem sweetheart." He laid a kiss on my temple.

Tyler came over to us. "How are you feeling?"

"Better."

"Good. Do you feel up to participating?"

"Can I see how I feel for a bit and try later on?" I asked.

"Of course."

"Thank you."

The rest of the day ran smoothly. I took part in a bit of final rehearsals but had to sit down after a short while. Jake kept watching me all morning to see how I was. Tyler dismissed us for our lunch break just after midday. By then I'd had painkillers and was beginning to feel better.

"What is your plan for lunch? He's given us just over an hour." Jake asked as he stood next to me again.

"I want to go out, but I'm not too sure. I don't know where I'd like to go."

"Are you feeling well enough to go?" Concern was etched across his face.

67

"Well I'll need to be won't I? Otherwise how on Earth will I get myself home?" I laughed.

"Well I'd drive you home if you wanted it."

"Let's go out for lunch and see how that goes."

"Sure."

Together we walked through the polished lobby of the theatre and out onto the street. Turning right, we headed down the high street. There was a little café down that way that I loved and that was where I was leading Jake to.

It was a small little thing, not much room for tables. It had been the place I sought comfort in throughout college when I was stressed and didn't want to be cooped at home any longer then I had to be. I'd taken my old best friend there on weekends occasionally; it had slowly begun to become our main hang out space. The outside walls were painted gold, the trim painted cream. The front had two full size windows that showed off the full view outside. Granted the only thing you could see were the town hall and any pedestrians walking past.

The interior design was lovely and floral. Small tables were scattered around one side of the café. Each table had a floral patterned tablecloth on with hedgehog pattern place mats. The walls were decorated with various painting and framed photos of waterfalls and beach scenes. That was why I found it so peaceful when I was there. The counter was on the other side, tucked away in the corner with a doorway to the kitchen in the corner of it.

Jake and I sat on a table at the back of the room. Quiet. I needed quiet to keep my head straight and keep myself intact. The menu was small, but it was good. They did sausage rolls, pasties, baguettes, sandwiches and paninis. They served a small variety of hot drinks, with a fridge full of cold drinks next to the counter for you to select your own. I knew exactly what I'd be having: hot chocolate and a chicken, ham and onion panini. The staff in here knew me well, they also knew I ordered the same thing every time I was in here. Jake flicked his eyes over the menu.

"The usual Addison?" Kirsten asked.

Kirsten was the waitress who'd sat by my side while I cried during the tough times and had gotten herself into trouble for it. She was one of the kindest people I knew. She had black hair streaked with grey and her bright blue eyes had started to darken over the last couple of years. Stress and pain didn't ever bring that woman down and I admired her so much for her strong spirit. She had a bubbly personality and would always try her best to bring a smile to the faces of everyone who ate in the café.

I lifted my eyes to look at her. "Of course. What else would I have?" I laughed.

"You're right hun, you never change. You do you." She noted my order down on her little order notepad before turning to Jake. I kicked his ankle from beneath the table. He clicked out of the reverie he'd been trapped in.

"I'd like the Meaty Baguette please and a latte."

"Anything else at all?" Kirsten asked us.

"No thank you."

Kirsten turned on her heel and carried our order to the kitchen. Shortly after we heard the sound of her frothing milk on the wan of the coffee machine. She filled the group head with coffee grounds and turned on the machine. I watched as she filled two espresso cups before pouring one into the bottom of a latte glass. She poured the milk into the glass and scooped out the froth with a teaspoon and placed it on top. To make my hot chocolate she mixed milk and hot chocolate powder together before heating it up using the wand again. She poured the chocolatey hot milk into a big cappuccino cup, put both on saucers and carried them over.

I smiled gratefully and the smell of chocolate.

"Mmm, thank you." I said, inhaling the smell from the wafting steam.

"You're welcome. Your food will be ready soon."

"You come here a lot?" Jake asked as he raised an eyebrow and took a sip of his latte. I always let my hot chocolate cool down slightly before I drank it so I wouldn't burn my tongue.

"I used to all the time through college. This place was where I'd come to relieve my stress. Kirsten, our waitress, was always the one who'd sit and listen or help me find solutions to what had gone wrong." I explained, gesturing to the walls around us.

"I'm glad you had a place to escape to."

Moments of silence passed before Kirsten brought us out our food. My eyes widened at the sight of food and my stomach growled in agreement.

"Thanks Kirsten" I called to her already retreating figure.

Jake had obviously been desperate for food too because he'd already started eating into his baguette. I picked up my knife and cut diagonally into my panini. *Mmm.* I took a bite and moaned at the different tastes on my tongue.

"Did you just have a foodgasm?" Jake asked, laughing.

"Maybe. You have sauce on you face." I pointed out.

"That's fine, I'll get it off once I'm finished."

Without responding, I carried on eating. Our time was running out so I began eating a little bit faster. I finished before Jake did so I went to get a couple of napkins so he could wipe his face when he was finished. Passing him the napkins, I sat back down. I sipped at my drink while I waited for him. He wiped his face with the napkins before gulping down the rest of his latte. I finished my hot chocolate then I went to find Kirsten to pay.

After I'd paid, with Jake protesting the whole time, we made our way back to work, hand in hand. He had his fingers laced through mine. Electricity pulsed through my veins, my heart filling with lust. Slowly strolling back to the theatre, I watched all the wildlife around us. I watched the trees dancing in the wind and butterflies flapping about around us. Bees pollinated every flower, their floral scent filling the air. Wind stroked every petal of each flower, every leaf on each tree. Dogs barked at each other as people walked them too closely to one another.

We got back to work in just enough time to spare. Most people had already come back if they hadn't stayed.

"One final rehearsal and then it'll be show time." Freddy announced. "From the top please."

So we ran through our final rehearsal.

Chapter 10

Opening night.

Tonight was our first performance of Cinderella. Holy crap was I nervous. I was shaking when I woke up that morning. My anxiety was at its peak already, heaven help me before I went onstage. Mum had booked herself a seat to watch so I felt more pressure on my shoulders to make her proud. I showered and dried my hair before plaiting it and going down for breakfast. Well, considering it was more midday, it was more like lunch at this point.

"Good luck for tonight darling." Mum said as she looked up from the soup she was stirring on the stove top. That would be what we'd reheat when we got home tonight. I was too full of nerves to eat anything now.

"Thanks mum. Is that for when we get back tonight?" I asked, gesturing to the soup.

"It will be. What are you having for lunch?"

"I'm not hungry." I told her.

"You need something. You missed breakfast and you won't have any dinner until late tonight so you're having something."

Sometimes my mum was so stubborn. I was happy I hadn't received that gene from her.

"I'm too nervous mum and if I eat I'll be sick. I don't want to relive what happened last time I went onstage. Remember how I was sick last time?"

"You won't be sick honey. You're going to be my brave girl and you're going to ace this performance tonight."

"Mum, did you really say I'll 'ace' it?" I laughed.

"Yes, isn't that what you kids say these days?"

"Yes but no."

"How can it be both?"

"Because it's weird when parents say it."

"Alright then." We stood in silence for few moments before mum spoke up. "Oi you cheeky mare, you forgot to tell me what you want for lunch." She scolded as she nudged my ribs playfully.

"Something small if you're forcing me to have something."

"My tomato pasta?"

"Too filling."

"A bowl of curly fries?" Now that was something I could never turn down.

"Yes please."

Mum walked over to the freezer while I turned the dial on the oven to preheat. It took a while to heat up before we could put my fries in.

"Go watch a film or something, it'll take your mind off it a bit."

"Ok mum." I kissed her cheek briefly and went through to the living room. I turned on Netflix and was half an hour in when she brings out my curly fries. "Thank you." She passed me the bottle of ketchup. I drizzled some across the top of the bowl of chips. Mum came and sat on the sofa beside me whilst I ate.

"You'll need to leave soon sweetie so you aren't late." I checked my phone.

"Shoot, is that really the time?"

"Yeah."

"I'll see you later then mum. I love you." I said as I ran to get my shoes on.

"Good luck!" Mum called as I left the house. I ran to the bus to make it on time.

"Addison!" Freddy exclaimed as I arrived to the theatre. "You alright? You look really nervous."

"Oh I am." I watched as his face spread into a grin.

"You'll do great, have some confidence in yourself."

"That's exactly what I *don't* have." I told him.

"You will."

We spent the afternoon double checking the lighting and moving the scenery to the correct angles and markers for the opening scenes. The further through the day we got, the more anxious I became. I tried taking deep breath, but they weren't really doing very much. I tried thinking of other things, not the show, but it didn't help when everyone kept asking if I was ready for the show. I wanted to scream at everyone to go away but thought against it. All I needed was some peace to get to grips with my emotions.

Before I knew it, evening came and people were starting to arrive. I heard echoes of chatter and commotion from behind the curtain. I was stood on the side of the stage in my first costume, ready to go on for my first scene. Creeping across the stage, I took a peek at how many people were in the audience. We were almost full of people. I felt sweat beading my forehead. Freddy came over after half an hour.

"Showtime people!"

This was it.

The day, the moment I'd been dreading.

Our opening performance.

I had to go up in front of loads of people and try to keep it together. I felt a panic attack rising up my throat. The curtains were raised and the performance began. They watched Ella growing up and I heard a few sobs when her father died. Her step sisters kicked her out her own room and that was that.

"Ella, your room is the biggest so give it up for your sisters." Lady Tremaine demanded.

I looked up at her from my place on the floor, soot covered my face from the fire.

"So what room will I move to? Am I swapping rooms with them?" I asked her as I stood up.

"You'll have the attic."

I looked at her with upset and confusion. "Oh. But there is no bed up there?"

"Take your mattress up with you. Get it done by midday tomorrow."

Over the course of the "day", I moved all my belongings to the attic. Anastasia was kind enough to help me. Then it was the ball. Ella, Cinderella as they'd renamed her, was left behind until her fairy godmother appeared. She performed her spell and then I twirled around and around until my ragged dress turned into my gorgeous ball gown.

It was a gorgeous baby blue silk with thin shoulder straps and a balloon skirt. Butterflies were embroidered in its bodice. I had on white silk shoes.

I arrived at the ball and found myself in the company of the prince. I felt so honoured to meet him outside the ballroom.

"Would you like a dance?" He asked, bowing and extending his hand out to me. I took it and he placed one hand on my waist. We waltzed through to the ballroom and joined the other dancers. I danced with Prince Charming until the spell had begun to wear off.

Panicking, I said "I have to go. Goodbye!"

"But why? Where are you going?" Prince Charming called as he ran out the ballroom with me.

The rest of the performance ran without a hitch. My anxiety and stage fright faded the longer I was up on the stage. Jake found me after the show had finished and scooped me into a hug.

"You were brilliant!" He said as he picked me up and spun me around.

"Thanks."

"We're doing more shows together, me and my girl."

He smiled and leant down to press his lips to mine. I parted my lips and he deepened our kiss. My hand wrapped round his neck and he gripped onto my waist tighter.

That was how we started a career in theatre together. He'd built up my confidence since I met him and he'd helped me push through every time we were on stage together.

We were going up in flames burning with desire for each other.

.

Ingram Content Group UK Ltd.
Milton Keynes UK
UKHW020046210623
423745UK00014B/397